Edwin Leigh

Hillard's Primer

Edwin Leigh

Hillard's Primer

ISBN/EAN: 9783337327392

Printed in Europe, USA, Canada, Australia, Japan

Cover: Foto ©Andreas Hilbeck / pixelio.de

More available books at **www.hansebooks.com**

HILLARD'S

PRIMER.

EDITED, IN

PRONOUNCING ORTHOGRAPHY.

By EDWIN LEIGH.

NEW YORK:
TAINTOR BRO'S, MERRILL & CO.
BOSTON: WILLIAM WARE & CO.
(*Successors to BREWER & TILESTON.*)
1877.

PRONOUNCING ORTHOGRAPHY.

——oo꞉o̶꞉oo——

THIS new adaptation of our printed to our spoken language, for the use of the learner, was first published and illustrated in a pamphlet entitled " Pronouncing Orthography, by Edwin Leigh, St. Louis, Missouri ; 1864."

For a more full account of it, its history, the serious evils to which it owes its origin, and its fitness as a practical remedy for those evils, see the second edition, entitled " Pronouncing Orthography Explained and Exemplified." A copy will be sent to any one who may request it by letter. Direct to E. Leigh, care of the publishers of this book.

But its essential features may be seen in this book. While the common spelling is preserved unchanged, the pronunciation of each word is exactly indicated. This is done by using a special form of a letter for each sound of it, and printing the silent or unsounded letters in a lighter type.

If the light letters seem too light to the eye accustomed to our Roman print, they are not too light for the learner, who needs to distinguish them as silent letters. No time or pains has been spared to secure the best forms of letters and make the best use of them, so that they may be sufficiently distinct for the learner, without changing materially the familiar aspect of the word or page.

This result of the labors of years is commended to the friends of our country and of education.

Any teacher can use this book with advantage to himself and pupils by adopting the plan of instruction indicated on pages 1 to 6 of the Primer.

LESSON I.

man	book	and	it
child	I see	the	is

I see a man.   It is a man.

I see a child.   It is a child.

I see a book.   It is a book.

I see a man, a child, and a book.

LESSON II.

boy   ball   cap   his
do   not   you   yes

See the boy.
See the ball.
It is his ball.
See his cap.
Is it his cap?
Yes, it is his cap.

Do you see the boy? Do you see his cap and his ball?

LESSON III.

word   hear   hark   can
black   loud   say   in

boy See the word! It is boy. It is in the book.

Hark! I say boy. Do you hear the word I say?

Yes, I hear the word you say. It is loud. I hear it. I can not see it.

The word in the book is black. I see it. I can not hear it.

LESSON IV.

| where | now | or | us |
| picture | let | me | of |

ball

cap

Now see the words ball and cap.

Hark! Hear me say cap, ball, boy.

See the picture of a boy, his cap, and his ball.

I see the picture. I see the words. I hear the words.

Do you see a boy? Where? Is it a boy, or a picture of a boy?

LESSON V.

Hark! Do you hear me say

be   bay   bar

he   hay   ha

e   a   a

It is be bay bar, he hay ha, e a a, e a a.

I say be he e, bay hay a, bar ha a, e a a.

Look! Hark! Now I say

er   no   do

ner   so   to

θ   ω   θ

I say er ner e, no so o, do to e, e o e. Now let us all say e a a, e o e.

look   will   may   all

LESSON VI.

Now hark! and hear me say

| fare | far | fur | war |
| care | car | cur | nor |

a ɑ u θ

Do you say ar ar ur or? No, it is a ɑ u θ.

Is it war nor or? No, it is war nor θ, a ɑ u θ.

See the signs! Hear the sounds!

| sign | point | sound | pure |
| ice | oil | our | use |

i oi ou u

I point to the signs i oi ou u in the book. Let us all sound i oi ou u, i oi ou u.

| they | long | sing | are |

LESSON VII.

Look! See the words and signs

| heat | mate | care | far |
| hit | met | cat | fast |

e   a   a   a

i   e   a   a

Hark! Hear me! I say heat hit e i, mate met a e, care cat a a, far fast a a, e i a e a a a a.

Hear the sounds e a a a. They are long, I sing them e a a a.

Now hear the sounds i e a a. They are short and sharp. Speak them quick, i e a a.

Sing e a a a. Now speak quick and sharp it et at at, i e a a.

them   short   sharp   speak

LESSON VIII.

Hark! Now you hear me say

cur	ner	hole	move
cut	not	whole	wolf

ꙋ θ ꙩ ϑ

u o ꚍ ꚙ

You may point to the signs u θ ꙩ θ, u o o o, and we will all sound u θ ꙩ θ, u o o o.

Now I know ei ae aa a a u u θo oo θo, i oi ou u.

quick	here	more	know

LESSON IX.

Now we will all say we ye he wheel, way yea hay whale.

You can say we wi, ye yi, he hi, whe whi. Can you say w y h wh?

Here are the words and signs

| we | ye | he | wheel |
| way | yea | hay | whale |

w y h wh

I can speak the words. I do not know the sounds. They are hard.

I will learn them, and then you can hear me say them.

learn   them   hard   these

LESSON X.

Look! here are more to learn.

m	seem	m	m	m	me
	ham-	m	m	m	mer
n	sun	n	n	n	not
	ban-	n	n	ŋ	ner
ŋ	sing-	ŋ	ŋ	ŋ	er
	fin-	ŋ	ŋ	ŋ	ger

My lips do not move while I say m m m. I keep my tongue still and sound n n n. It is not em en eᴅ, or mu nu. It is m n ᴅ.

| while | move | lips | my |

LESSON XI.

l	fail	l	l	l	lot
	mal-	l	l	l	let
r	bor-	r	r	r	row
	hur-	r	r	r	ried
r	her	r	r	r	earn
	cur	r	r	r	urn

Do I say el el el, ar ar ar? No it is l l l, r r r. You do not move your tongue when you say r r r.

But I do move my tongue when I say r r r; it is ur ur ur.

| tongue | when | still | keep |

LESSON XII.

v f	love	v	v	v	vine
	loaf	f	f	f	fish
th th	with	th	th	th	this
	oath	th	th	th	thin
s s	scis-	s	s	s	sors
	us	s	s	s	so
s sh	pleas-	s	s	s	ure
	wish	sh	sh	sh	ship

Hark! Hear v th s s! I sing them; you hear my voice.

Now hear f th s sh. I can not sing them; you do not hear my voice; all you hear is my breath, f th s sh.

Now sound v th s s, f th s sh. Now say v f th th s s s sh.

breath   your   voice   but

LESSON XIII.

b p	rub	b	b	b	boy
	lip	p	p	p	pin
d t	bad	d	d	d	dig
	hot	t	t	t	top
g ch	age	g	g	g	gem
	each	ch	ch	ch	chin
g c	dog	g	g	g	get
	arc	c	c	c	cat

Hark! I say b d g g, and you hear my voice.

Do you hear my voice when I say p t ch c? No, it is your breath.

Look! When I say b b b p p p, I move my lips; but I do not say be pe, or bu pu. It is b b p p.

Now all sound b p d t g ch g c, b d g g, p t ch c.

LESSON XIV.

To preserve the Orthography unchanged, a few duplicate signs are used in this book. They are here printed in pairs for comparison, reference, and practice.

a	may	u	nut	t	slept
ɑ	thay	ʋ	love	ꝺ	hopeꝺ
e	men	i	mine	ɡ	gem
ɐ	many	y	my	j	joy
a	care	oi	boil	ʋ	live
ɛ	there	oy	boy	ꝙ	of
ɵ	nor	oṷ	house	f	half
ɑ	gnaw	ow	how	ꝝ	laugꝝ
o	not	ʉ	use	s	rise
ɑ	what	w	ewe	z	prize
o	wolf	u	blue	s	vase
u	put	ʋ	blew	c	face
o	reod	i	pin	c	cat
u	rude	ė	been	k	kite
ɯ	grew	y	lynx	q	quill
w	wit	ʋ	quit	ʋ	one

LESSON XV.

There are, in our language, a few cases in which a single letter stands for a double sound, or diphthong, or even a triple or triphthongal sound.

i   isle   The *i* in *isle*, like *ai* in *aisle*, is not a simple sound, but consists of the two sounds, — *a* and ai   aisle   *i*, joined in one.

w   yew   The *w* in *yew*, like *u* in *use*, consists of three yew   yew   sounds, — y, i, oo, joined in one.

w   flew   In *flew*, *tune*, *due*, *sue*, and in all cases of the same class, the consonant *y* sound is not ew   flew   heard, but only the vowel i joined to oo.

o   one   The *o* in *one*, like the *wo* in *won*, stands wo   won   for two sounds, — w in *we*, and o in *son*.

x   tax   I use the Italic form *x* to denote ks or cs, where x stands for these sounds, reserving the ks   tacks   Roman form x for gz in such words as *exert*.

r   cur   The *r* in *far*, *wary*, *very*, is the simple consonant *r*. But the *r* in *flour* is not. Like the ur   cur   *er* in *flower*, it consists of two sounds, — *u* and *r*. To denote this double sound *ur*, a peculiar form of *r* is used in words of this class.

The following words are therefore printed thus: —

aisle yew flew one cur, instead of
aisle yew flew wone cur

For more full explanations of the preceding lessons, see page ii. See also pages 1–6 of the Primer.

LESSON XVI.

Of the capitals used in this book, the common Roman forms are appropriated to these sounds:—

In	I i	An	A a	On	O o
We	W w	Ye	Y y	He	H h
Me	M m	Not	N n	Let	L l
Rat	R r	For	F f	Be	B b
Pen	P p	Do	D d	To	T t
Joy	J j	Go	G g	Cat	C c
Kate	K k				

For the other sounds, the following special forms are used:—

Ail	A a	Art	A a	All	A a
Or	Θ θ	Old	O o	End	E e
Ice	I i	One	Ʊ ʊ	So	S s
She	Sh sh	Gem	G g		

Lessons XV. and XVI. are not really lessons for the learner, being intended rather for the eye of the parent or teacher. The capitals, like the numerals, will be best taught as they occur in the reading lessons, though the above table may be used for review and practice.

The duplicate signs (Lesson XIV.), and indeed all the Sound Lessons may be better taught with the aid of the Sound Charts, and separate letters on cards, prepared for the purpose to accompany this book. The teacher will also find the blackboard of great service.

THE PRIMER,

OR

FIRST READER. — NEW SERIES.

BY G. S. HILLARD AND L. J. CAMPBELL.

TO THE TEACHER.

THIS edition of Hillard's Primer is an exact copy, in pronouncing type, of the one hitherto in use; only, the last five lessons, having been in smaller print, have here a few words and their arrangement slightly changed, and are extended over seven pages instead of six. In all other respects it corresponds with the former, line to line, and page to page. It may therefore be used without disadvantage, even in the same class where a part of the scholars have the other edition; or this may be used to study the lessons which are to be read at the recitation from that.

Being printed in the common spelling, with the type so slightly changed, it may, of course, be used by any teacher in the same way as he now uses the old edition. But it is not particularly adapted to

THE A B C METHOD.

This mode of teaching is now generally disapproved by the best and most experienced educators; though there are some teachers, who, for various reasons, still practise it.

To teach the letters by their names, and reading by spelling out the words, is not a good plan, even in truly alphabetic languages like the Spanish or Italian; but in our language it is fraught with mischief, the letters being so irregularly used, and the printed language being, for the learner, quite as distinct from the spoken as is the case in the Chinese. It has been said with truth, that the six months, on the average, which are spent in learning the names of the letters, are worse than wasted in acquiring what is a hindrance rather than a help. And the years which are afterwards to so great an extent occupied with the stupefying toil of spelling out groups of letters that are no guide to the spoken words they stand for, are also wretchedly misused.

What connection is there between the names *double-you, aye, ess,* and the spoken word **was** ? between the names *eye, ess,* and the word **is** ? There is not a sound in either of the names that is heard in the words. There is no more relation between these printed and spoken words than there is between *lbs. etc. dwt.* and **pounds, and so forth, pennyweight.** I may as rationally say ($) *ess and two vertical parallel lines through it,* **dollars,** or (£) *ell and one horizontal line through it,* **pounds,** as to say *eye ess,* **is.** It would be quite as sensible to spell **and** by describing the curves and crossings of the character &. The student of Latin does the very same thing when he spells *e t,* **and;** or *e r a t,* **was;** or *e s t,* **is.** It is exactly the same; for Horace Mann was right when he said, " There are two English languages, — one for speaking, the other for writing and printing; and I believe the mastering of these to be more difficult for children than that of two languages wholly distinct and separate from each other."

This book, therefore, has not been adapted to teach on the *Aye Bee Cee, bee aye dee* **bad,** plan, but rather to avoid the absurdities and evils of that plan, and (while it secures the great benefits which have been obtained by the use of the phonetic method and a regular print) to retain the advantages of the best methods now in use. One of the best of these is

THE WORD METHOD.

All the lessons in this book are arranged to be taught, and may perhaps be best taught, by dictation and concert-reading on the word-plan. At least, each lesson should be read in this way once on assigning it to the class, and a few times at the recitation-hour.

Let the teacher, in Lesson I., read aloud to the class, *I see a man* (pointing to the words as he reads), and let the pupil or pupils then read one sentence in concert with the teacher. Then the pupil may read the sentence alone, after the teacher has read it to him. Or the words, *I see,* may be dictated and read first, and then the words, *a man,* and then the whole sentence, *I see a man;* and so on with the remaining sentences of Lesson I. and of all the other lessons.

By this method, each word will be taught from the teacher's lips; the child will imitate the teacher's speech, will pronounce and articulate as he does, and give the same inflections. And the more accuracy, precision, spirit, and life the teacher gives to his own reading, the more will be caught and acquired by the pupil.

Each word, too, will be taught in its connection as it is used in the sentence, and will not be an abstract, unmeaning, lifeless thing, creating only dulness, but will be full of life and meaning, and awaken such an interest, that, without special effort to learn the separate words, the child will become familiar with each and all of them before he or the teacher is aware of it.

If, however, the teacher prefer, the words may first be taught in the columns at the head or foot of the lessons, and then used in reading. But these columns are designed rather for review and practice, to test the pupil's knowledge of the words, and to perfect him in it. Even the experienced phonetic teacher will do well to make no little use of the word-plan, as it will aid in giving fluency, naturalness, and expression to the reading, and thus prevent some faults which the exclusive use of the phonetic method is apt to foster. Phonetic and word teaching are by no means inconsistent with each other. They may be used together in perfect harmony, each for its own special purpose. So also

OBJECT TEACHING

Should be associated with all the lessons. This may be done by the use of the engravings, and, as far as they can be obtained, of the objects which they represent, or any others referred to in the reading-matter. Some of the ways in which it may be done to advantage are indicated in Lessons II., III., and IV., on pages ii. and iii. of the Word Lessons. To the wide-awake mind of the earnest teacher, other ways will readily suggest themselves.

THE PHONIC METHOD.

This term has been applied to various adaptations of the phonetic principle, to books printed in the common orthography, without any special notation of the different sounds of the letters, or with only a partial and imperfect one. All that need be said of them here is included in the following remarks on

THE PHONETIC METHOD.

When, instead of teaching whole words, as **know, knife**; or spelling them by the names of the letters, as, *k-n-o-w*, **know**; *k-n-i-f-e*, **knife**; we spell them by sound, as,

kn ow   kn i fe   pſh ɑw   gn ɐw

we teach phonetically. , This is teaching by sound; it is not spelling words, it is sounding words: the Germans call it *lautiren*.*

To teach the Primer Lessons phonetically, consider the words on page 7 to be divided into their several sounds, and teach them thus : —

s o	so	g o	go	n o	no
h e	he	a m	am	i s	is
w e	we	in	in	o n	on

Or teach the words on page 31 thus : —

b ee s	h i ve	s ti ŋg	ḷoo k
li ve	c ʋ me	w or k	b oo k
d o ll	m ay	n eʋ	h ea d

and proceed in like manner with all the lessons as if they were so divided. The words in the reading-lessons may be taught in the same way.

---

* lɑ-ut-ɪ′ren (by Worcester's key löût-ē′rĕn)

THE WORD LESSONS, I. to IV., *look* harder than the first few lessons of the Primer. *Are* they actually so ? Is it harder on the word-plan to learn the words *child, book, picture,* than it is to learn *so, go, no ?* A child will learn to know a sofa as quick as he will know a chair, or a house as quick as a post, though it is a much longer and larger thing. So he will learn to say *mamma* as readily as *is* or *at,* though it is a longer word, and has more sounds and syllables. In fact, cannot a child learn, on the word-plan, the words *man, book, and, it,* quicker than he can *he, we, an, in ?* The very difference between the larger and smaller words will aid him in his first efforts. The Word and Sound Lessons, though they look more difficult, are constructed as they are, because they are believed to be easier and better for both teacher and pupil.

THE SOUND LESSONS, V. to XVI., pages vi. to xvi., are designed not so much to be read and learned by the pupil as to guide the teacher and pupils to the practice of vocal drill in the elementary sounds. Were every teacher familiar with the phonetic method, and skilled in enunciating the simple sounds and analyzing words by sound (sounding words *), only the classified lists of large letters (signs) would be printed, with the key-words connected with them. But as few have had experience in phonetic teaching, or can readily obtain instruction in it, these lessons are so arranged as to be self-teaching; and it is believed, that, by the use of them, any teacher and class can go on, step by step, to the successful practice of this admirable method.

The main object of the first Sound Lesson (V.) is to have teacher and pupil sound aloud in the right way, and in their natural order, the simple vowel-sounds *ee ay ah aw oh oo.* So the object of each succeeding lesson is, that the sounds to which it relates be sounded in the right way, in their natural order and relations.

Let the teacher first read the Sound Lessons through in order; read them aloud many times, and with spirit, freedom, and expres-

---

* The observant reader will notice the distinction made between *spelling* words and *sounding* them; and between the twenty-six *letters* of the alphabet, whether silent, or however sounded, and the *signs,* or special forms appropriated to denote particular sounds.

sion: he will thus soon become familiar with the elementary sounds, and the order and manner in which they are arranged to be taught and practised.

The key-words are a sufficient guide to the right sounds: * the errors to be avoided are perhaps sufficiently indicated in the lessons themselves, as are the different ways of practising the exercises. Always point to the sign at the moment it is sounded.

Some teachers may prefer to teach the sounds first, without the book or any printed letters; and, after the pupil has become familiar with the sounds, to teach them in connection with the printed signs. It seems best, however, to teach them together from the first.

It will be well to commence the Sound Lessons in connection with the reading-lessons, either at the same recitation-hour, or at another hour of each day, and, after the Sound Lessons are mastered, to practise all the elements in regular order at every recitation: it will be a minute's time well spent in vocal gymnastics.

If the child has already "learned his letters," and formed the habit of "spelling words," he should be taught the difference between spelling by names and spelling by sound, and made to confine himself to the latter while using this book.

THE NUMERALS and figures should be taught as they occur in the lessons, and reviewed from time to time by turning over the leaves, or by the use of the black-board.

CHARTS of Sound Lessons, printed in large type for class exercises, have been prepared in a style and at a price designed to make them generally acceptable and useful.

A *Second* Primary Reading Book in Pronouncing Orthography will be ready for the pupil when he has finished this book.

Teachers using this book will confer a favor by communicating to the author the results (favorable or otherwise) of their trial of it.

---

* In Lesson X., first say *seem*; then, without opening or moving the lips, repeat *m* three times; then say *me*. So repeat *n* three times without moving the tongue. Do the same with all the other sounds excepting l oi ou ŭ, p t ch k, and b d j g; though b d j g may be sounded imperfectly without moving the articulating organs.

The more difficult sounds, w y h wh (Lesson IX.), may be passed over the first time going through the lessons.

LESSON I.

so   go   no

I go.   I go so.   So I go.

LESSON II.

he   am   is

we   in   on

Am I on?   I am on.   Is he on?

He is on.

Is he in?

We go on.

So we go.

LESSON III.

an	at	by	er
ox	it	my	us

An ox.

So it is.

Go on, ox.

Is it my ox?

Go by my ox.   It is my ox.

Ox, go by us.   Go by, ox.

LESSON IV.

be	as	up	do
me	ye	if	to

He is up.

He is on.

Do go on.

So be it.

Go by me.

If ye go on,　Do go by me.

Is he to go on?　He is to go on.

LESSON V.

It is he.　Is it he or I?

Is it I? No.　Is it an ox? No.

We do so.　Go on or go up.

Do as we do.　We do go on.

LESSON VI.

cat	cap	fed	pig
hat	can	hen	fly
rat	fat	run	my

A hat.   It is my hat.

A cat.   Is it my cat?

A rat.   Run, rat, run.

A cap.   It is my cap.

A hen.   Can a hen fly?

A pig.   I fed a fat pig.

LESSON VII.

had	dog	big	the
man	box	hut	old
men	tin	jug	owl

A man. The man had a dog.

A dog. Dog, go to the man.

A box. It is a tin box.

A jug. It is a big jug.

An owl. An owl can fly.

A hut. It is an old hut.

LESSON VIII.

and   see   pin   boy

the   top   spin   you

Is it a top?

We see a boy

and a top.

The boy can

spin the top.

Can you spin it? I can spin

my top.   See the top go.

LESSON IX.

old   get   did   for

ran   dog   his   of

A big dog.   An old rat.

I see a dog and a rat.

It is my dog.
Did the dog get
the rat? No; for
the rat ran.
The rat is in.

LESSON X.

sat	not	paw	you
pat	yes	lap	boy

Do you see a boy?
Yes, I can see a
boy and a dog.
I can see the paw
of the dog.
Is it on the boy's lap?
Dog, go and get me a rat.

LESSON XI.

wet	will	back	Ann
too	with	are	Ned

Do you see the dog? Yes.

Ann is on the dog's back.

Ned is by Ann.   We see Ned.

Is it my dog? It is not my dog. It is his dog.

Can the dog go with Ann? Yes, the dog can go with Ann.

Ned will go with Ann too.

Ann will not get wet.

If Ned and Ann are to go, I will go.

LESSON XII.

bad	fat	fan	rap
had	mat	man	has
lad	bat	pan	sad

LESSON XIII.

that	when	she	cry
them	why	shy	try

Do you see the cat? She will try to get a rat.

She is not a bad cat.

Can she get a rat? She will try to get the fat rat.

Why is that rat so shy? Can he see the cat?

When will the cat get them? Run, rat, run.

LESSON XIV.

bed	get	met	peg
fed	let	yet	beg
red	pet	net	leg

LESSON XV.

was	nest	sly	your
what	eggs	but	have

I fed my hen. She is a pet. Your pet is not my pet. The sly cat is my pet.

Your old hen has a nest, but my cat has a bed.

We have no nest for a cat.

LESSON XVI.

What do we see?
We see a nest.
Eggs are in the
nest.
It is not the nest
of a hen.

Do not let your sly cat see
the nest.

LESSON XVII.

bid	bit	pig	lip
did	hit	dig	skip
hid	sit	fig	whip

LESSON XVIII.

then	cat	shall	fast
this	give	saw	last

Is it a pig? Yes, and a man. It is his pig. It is his dog, too.

The pig can run fast. Can the dog run as fast as the pig? Yes, but the pig can not run as fast as the dog.

The pig is not fat. He is to be fed. What shall we give him to eat?

LESSON XIX.

O, what a bad boy this is!

Do not hit the dog.

It is sad to see a boy so bad as this boy.

LESSON XX.

got	pot	hop	nod
hot	spot	shop	hog
lot	shot	rob	fox

LESSON XXI.

stag	hill	sees	own
stand	still	shoot	show

This is a stag. He can run fast.

He will not stand still in that spot when he sees a man or a dog.

The man can not shoot the stag, for he will run to the hill.

LESSON XXII.

You are my own boy. Run to me. Can you not? Try. Do not cry. See the top. If you can get to me, you shall have it.

LESSON XXIII.

bug	cut	gun	dust
dug	hut	sun	dusk
mug	nut	drum	just

LESSON XXIV.

tree	now	left	one
men	down	axe	two

See this tree and the two men. The men will cut down the tree. You can cut down a tree with an axe.

One of the men has a gun. You can not see his gun, for he

left it in his hut. That is his dog, Skip.

His boy, Tom, has a drum. We can see Tom and his drum.

Two boys are with Tom.

LESSON XXV.

bar	jar	hard	arm
car	star	yard	farm
far	dark	barn	harm

LESSON XXVI.

cow	how	out	our
bow	town	pout	sour

Two cows are in the yard by the barn. A boy is at the bars. He has just let the cows in to the yard.

When the cows go out of the yard, the boy will have to let down the bars.

This is a farm, and it is not far from a town. It is our farm.

When we are in the town, we can go out to the farm in a car.

It is not dark yet, nor is it dusk. When it is dark, we can see the stars.

LESSON XXVII.

all	fall	small	paw
ball	hall	salt	saw
call	tall	raw	draw

LESSON XXVIII.

bell	gruff	dress	back
tell	stuff	press	black
mill	stiff	grass	stuck

This boy has two small pups
in his arms. He will not let
them fall.

It is Ned's dog, and the pups are his too.

Ann sits on the grass. **Ann** is not so tall as Ned.

I see the pup's paw. It is on Ned's arm. Do you see it?

My dog is a black dog. We call him Muff. Ann saw Muff at the mill. She will try to get on his back.

LESSON XXIX.

bank	ink	ring	thing
thank	brink	bring	long
drink	think	hang	song

LESSON XXX.

oil	broil	boy	joy
toil	spoil	cloy	toy
fish	good	fine	they
must	hook	sport	there

Ned and Dick are on the bank.
See them! they are just on the
brink. Ned has a fine fish
on his hook. Will he let it hang

on the hook? No, he will have
to get it off now, but that will
not be hard to do.

Bring it to me, Ned. Thank
you. How long it is ! This fish
is good to broil.

It is fine sport for boys to
fish. It is not toil, but play.

Ned is a good boy. We must
give him a toy.

LESSON XXXI.

came	same	lake	gave
game	pale	take	brave
lame	made	late	grape
name	make	slate	mate

LESSON XXXII.

here　　　play　　　what　　　girl

Here are two girls and a boy at play.

What is the boy's name? Is it the same boy that we saw with the dog? No: this boy's name is Frank.

Frank can not see the girls now. Jane came up and gave him a tap. Then Jane ran.

They must not play at that game till it is late.

bees	hive	sting	lock
live	come	work	bock

A boy and a girl have come out to look at the bees. Bees live in a hive. They work hard. Can you tell me what they make? The bees will not sting the boy or the girl.

LESSON XXXIII.

care	fare	share	rare
bare	spare	scare	dare
doll	may	new	head

What a fine doll Ann has!

Ann, will you let us play with your doll?

Yes, if you will take good care of it.

I can spare my doll now, so you may play with it.

The doll has a new dress. It has a hat on its head. See its bare· arm.

Ann and the girls will go out to play, but they will not go far.

LESSON XXXIV.

time	side	rise	fire
crime	ride	wise	tire
mine	wide	white	hire
shine	like	kite	while

LESSON XXXV.

dry	try	fly	spy
cry	fry	sky	why
bells	put	house	glad

Fire! fire! fire! A cry of fire! A house is on fire. Run, men, and try to put out the fire.

See the fireman run.

The fire shines on all sides. All the while the bells ring.

I am glad the house is not mine.

It is a crime to set a house on fire.

A boy and a kite. He will fly it. It will rise far up in the sky.

Do you like to fly a kite? Yes, we do, when we have a fine kite like this.

LESSON XXXVI.

face	mice	age	large
pace	nice	rage	charge
place	slice	cage	change
race	twice	page	strange
horse	colt	bird	her

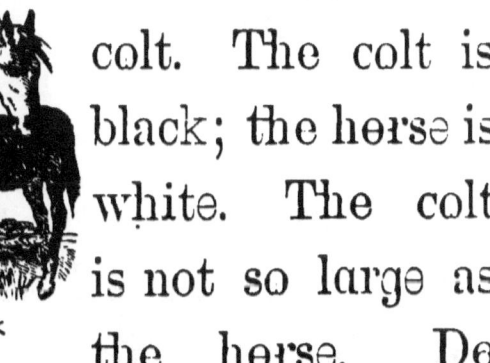

A horse and a colt. The colt is black; the horse is white. The colt is not so large as the horse. Do you see the face of the horse?

When the horse and colt run a race, they can run twice as fast as we can.

LESSON XXXVII.

Here is a bird in a cage. A girl stands by the cage.

It is not the girl's bird, but she has it in her charge.

The cage is the bird's house. Is not a cage a nice place for a bird?

Our cat likes to get mice. That is not strange, but I do not like to have her try to bite my pet bird.

LESSON XXXVIII.

broke	rose	home	hope
spoke	nose	stone	rope
yoke	those	more	smoke
one	once	jump	kind

It is fine sport for Ann to jump the rope. It makes her face as red as a rose.

I hope she will not jump too long at one time.

She must jump no more now, for she must go home.

Once Ann broke her rope. She spoke to me, and I let her take mine.

We must all be kind to our play mates.

LESSON XXXIX.

flute	cure	tune	tube
mute	pure	use	blue
few	dew	pew	stew
flew	blew	mew	view

LESSON XL.

air	found	day	ill
hear	sound	great	shrill

The sun is up. It is day now. Let us go out while the dew is on the grass.

We shall have a fine view. We can see the blue sky.

The air is pure; if we are ill it will cure us.

Far off we can hear a man play a tune on his flute. A flute is a long tube. I once blew into a flute. It was not mute then, for it gave out a shrill sound.

LESSON XLI.

four	their	went	kit tens
milk	wish	hurt	with out′

Jane Lee has a large cat. Her name is Tab. Tab has four kit tens. They are small yet, but they can lap milk out of a cup.

A few days a go'our large dog, Bose, saw the kittens at play. So he came up to them and stuck out his nose. Tab was by, and flew at him in a great rage.

Bose saw he must not do that. He did not wish to hurt Tab or her kittens; so he went off, and left them to have their play with out' his help.

LESSON XLII.

sir	from	says	who
say	stops	smith	shoe
lost	mind	tired	father
told	woods	asleep´	mother

This is the shop of a smith. The smith stops from his work to look at the boy, and to hear what he has to say. The great horse too looks at the boy. The boy says, "Can you shoe my horse, too, sir?"

Here is a boy who has lost his way. He went out to play. His mother told him not to go into the woods. But he did not mind her, and lost his way. At last he was tired out, and fell asleep. His father will soon find him.

LESSON XLIII.

sheep	holds	boat	wool
green	hands	swan	going
plant	waves	neck	feeding

This boat moves fast. In it you may go far from home. The waves do not run high now. The flags float in the air. Can you tell which way the boat is going? What kind of a boat do you call this?

Here is a large bird. It is a swan. The swan likes to swim. What a long neck!

A girl is feeding her pet sheep.
The sheep likes to eat the green
plant which the girl holds in her
hands. Can you tell me what men
do with the wool of the sheep?

LESSON XLIV.

come	John	rains	keep
a wake´	school	been	o ver

Here are two good girls just come
from school. It rains fast, but they
do not fear the rain. Do you think
they will get wet? Can you tell me

what the girl holds over her head to keep off the rain?

Little John has been a good boy all day. Now he is going to bed. Who takes care of little boys when they are a wake' or a sleep'? It is God who takes care of all.

LESSON XLV.

lost	sea	were	a bout'
held	roll	read	sis ter
boat	show	child	broth er
ship	would	splash	play ing

James Dale has a new book. He is glad to show it to his little brother and sis ter. In books we can read a bout' great and good men, and what they did long a go'.

This boy and his dog were playing on the deck of a ship, when the
ship gave a roll, and splash went the
child into the sea. At the same
time the dog sprang into the sea.
Some men got into a boat to try
to save the boy, who would have
been lost if his brave dog had not
held him up till the boat came.
How glad the men were to take
them into the boat!

LESSON XLVI.

day	talks	strong	visit
stay	walks	could	very
part	spade	should	friend
high	some	would	tosses

Little Ella has come to visit her friend Dora. She can stay all day, and they will have a fine time playing with their dolls.

Ella calls her doll Lady Jane.

She is very fond of Lady Jane, and talks to her as if the doll could hear what she says.

"Come, Lady Jane," says Ella, "let me see how well you can walk. You must walk like mamma'."

I think Lady Jane will not go far without' Ella's help.

Dora has a fine large doll. See how high she tosses it!

Here is a boy with a spade. What do you think he will do with it? This boy likes to work part of the time. It is good for boys to do some work. Work will make them strong. But boys must play too.

LESSON XLVII.

tell	lives	deal	ug ly
there	bear	pond	beast
where	most	snow	wa ter

What do you think of this beast? Is he not ug ly? He lives in the wa ter most of the time. Can you tell me his name?

Here is a great white bear. He lives far from us, in a place where there is a great deal of ice and snow.

James and his sister Jane have come down to the pond, where there are some swans. James is holding out his hand to the white swan.

LESSON XLII.

hands	look	sport	shadow
head	wolf	move	pa pa'
ears	chair	neck	mam ma'

Now we will have rare sport. Our pa pa' will play with us. He will make us a shadow on the wall with his hands.

Now, papa´, you can sit in the old arm-chair, and I will stand here by your side.

Look! what a large shadow it is! See how black it is!

It is like the head of a dog or a wolf. I can see its ears, and its nose, and its neck.

Papa´ can make the shadow move on the wall when he moves his hands. Now let me make one.

LESSON XLIII.

ship	dash	floats	sail
land	rock	blow	air
wind	sea	rude	earth
flag	seems	world	round

A ship is on the sea. Look at it. It will sail to a land far from ours. A flag floats in the air. Sail a way´, ship.

I hope no rude wind will blow the ship out of the way, and that the sea will not rise and dash it upon' a rock.

We live on the earth. The earth is not flat, as it seems to us to be, but round.

Men can sail round the earth, or world, in ships.

LESSON XLIV.

bloom	soon	boot	cool
gloom	moon	root	poor
room	noon	soot	fool
lose	near	flowers	hay mow
hold	fears	showing	ladder
there	wore	a way'	sister

This boy is on the hay mow in the barn. He has found a hen's nest. There are four eggs in it, and the boy holds one egg in his hand, which he is showing to his sister.

His little sister is on the ladder. She must hold fast so as not to fall.

It will soon be noon. You may put on your hat, and we will go out.

It is a hot day, so we will sit in the cool shade of the trees.

We can see the flowers in bloom and hear the little birds sing. When it is cool we will go back to the house.

We have cut down the trees that were near our house, for they made a dark shade, and there was a deep gloom in my room.

LESSON XLV.

The Little Dog.

What can you do? Let me see.
Walk on two legs, sir, like me?
Can you beg, and dance, and spring,
And your master's slip pers bring?

The Big Dog.

I can't do that; but care I take,
Into the house no thief shall break.

LESSON XLVI.

Snow Man.

See! a snow man! Run, boys, quick!
How he grasps his big thick stick!

Two whole days he's stood just so,
Yet hath never struck one blow.

Snow man, poor man, I'd never be
Holding a useless stick like thee.

www.ingramcontent.com/pod-product-compliance
Lightning Source LLC
Chambersburg PA
CBHW030009030726
47499CB00008B/2979